Mario & Baby Gia

BY
Mario Lopez

illustrated by
Maryn Roos

A Celebra Children's Book
A member of Penguin Group (USA) Inc.

For my girls, Mazza and Gia Francesca! And the two nana's, Elvia and Elaine. —M.L.

For my new baby cousins: Ender, Bo, and Seth —M.R.

CELEBRA CHILDREN'S BOOKS
A member of Penguin Group (USA) Inc.

Penguin Group (USA) Inc., 375 Hudson Street, New York, New York 10014, U.S.A.

Penguin Group (Canada), 90 Eglinton Avenue East, Suite 700, Toronto, Ontario M4P 2Y3, Canada (a division of Pearson Penguin Canada Inc.)

Penguin Books Ltd, 80 Strand, London WC2R ORL, England

Penguin Ireland, 25 St Stephen's Green, Dublin 2, Ireland (a division of Penguin Books Ltd)

Penguin Group (Australia), 250 Camberwell Road, Camberwell, Victoria 3124, Australia (a division of Pearson Australia Group Pty Ltd)

Penguin Books India Pvt Ltd, 11 Community Centre, Panchsheel Park, New Delhi - 110 017, India

Penguin Group (NZ), 67 Apollo Drive, Rosedale, Auckland 0632, New Zealand (a division of Pearson New Zealand Ltd.)

Penguin Books (South Africa) (Pty) Ltd, 24 Sturdee Avenue, Rosebank, Johannesburg 2196, South Africa

Penguin Books Ltd, Registered Offices: 80 Strand, London WC2R ORL, England

CIP Data is available.

Published in the United States by Celebra Children's Books,
a member of Penguin Group (USA) Inc.
375 Hudson Street, New York, New York 10014
www.penguin.com/youngreaders

Designed by Liz Frances

Manufactured in China   First Edition

ISBN 978-0-451-23417-9

1 3 5 7 9 10 8 6 4 2

It was only a few days until Mario's birthday and Mario couldn't wait! Where was his sister, Marissa? He wanted to tell her about his birthday party ideas.

"Marissa!" he called.

Marissa was playing with Cousin Rosie under the big tree in the backyard.

"No boys allowed, Mario!" Rosie and Marissa giggled.

Mario decided to go see what Chico was up to. Just as he was about to knock on the front door, Chico came outside.

"Chico! I was just—"

"I can't talk now," Chico interrupted. "I'm late for baseball practice!"

Hmmph. Mario crossed his arms.
Now what do I do? he said to himself.

"Mario! Is that you?" It was Nana, with his baby cousin. "You're just the person I was looking for! I need your help watching Gia while I do some baking. Can you help?"

Mario wasn't sure he wanted to watch Gia. He'd rather be playing catch with Chico, playing pretend with Marissa and Rosie, or planning his birthday party. Mario looked at Nana and Gia. He knew he should be responsible. "I can help you, Nana."

"Gia, are you excited to play with me?" Mario bent down to Gia's level.

Gia pointed her finger at Mario's nose. "Marigold!" Gia said.

"No, Gia. MA-RI-O. I'm Mario!"

"Marigold!"

"Hmmph." Mario frowned.

Mario took Gia to play in the backyard. Mario showed Gia how to throw the ball.

"Like this, Gia." Mario gently tossed the ball at Gia. Gia picked up the ball and threw it the opposite way.

"Ball!" Gia said. The dog ran after it, fetched it, and brought it back to Gia.

"Dog!"

"Throw it to me now," Mario said encouragingly.
This time, Gia threw it up over the fence.
"Gia!" Mario cried.
"Marigold!" Gia pointed at Mario.
"My name is Mario! MA-RI-O!"
"Marigold!"

"Nana, can we help you bake?" Mario asked when he took Gia inside.

"Why don't you give Gia her snack?" Nana said.

Mario sat Gia in her high chair and poured crackers in a bowl. Gia pulled Mario's hair.

Then, Gia turned the bowl upside down. Crackers scattered all over the floor.

"Bowl!"

"Gia! Why did you do that?" Mario quickly swept up the mess before the dog could eat it all.

Whatever Nana was making smelled delicious. Mario's
tummy grumbled. "Nana, are you sure I can't help you
bake?" Mario was hoping she'd let him lick the leftover batter.
   "Why don't you read Gia a story in the den?" Nana
suggested.

Mario looked over at Gia. She was wearing the
bowl as a hat.

"Marigold!" Gia said, pointing at Mario.

"My name is Marigold . . . I mean MARIO!"

Mario sat Gia next to him on the couch and opened up her favorite book.

"Book!" Gia said.

"Right, Gia, I'm going to read you a story."

Gia had other ideas. She grabbed the first page and pulled on it until it ripped.

"NO, Gia!" Mario crossed his arms. "Today was supposed to be a fun day but you're ruining it!"

"Book!" Gia said.

"I'm not reading a story to you. I'm too mad!"

Gia looked up at Mario's angry face. She scooted closer to Mario, reached up, and planted a kiss on Mario's cheek.

"Mario," Gia whispered. She snuggled into Mario's lap. "Story."

Mario couldn't help but smile. He put the book away and told his own story. He told Gia about playing pretend with his cousins, how Nana showed them how to cook, and how they set up their own restaurant in the backyard.

Mario told Gia about when he taught Marissa how to ride a bike, how she got right back on and tried again, even after Chico laughed at her for falling off. He told Gia about games of hide-and-go-seek outside and catching lightning bugs at night.

"You'll see. You're a part of our family. We'll teach you everything you need to know."

"Balloon!" Gia said.

"Balloon? Are you even listening, Gia?"

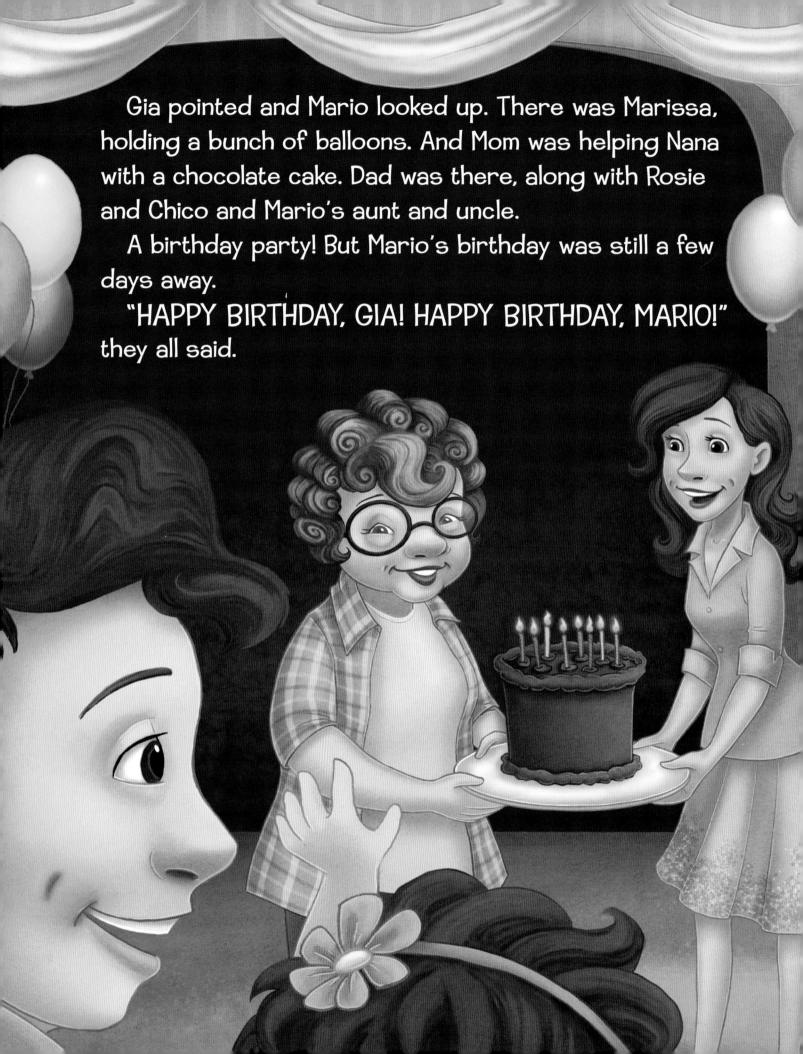

Gia pointed and Mario looked up. There was Marissa, holding a bunch of balloons. And Mom was helping Nana with a chocolate cake. Dad was there, along with Rosie and Chico and Mario's aunt and uncle.

A birthday party! But Mario's birthday was still a few days away.

"HAPPY BIRTHDAY, GIA! HAPPY BIRTHDAY, MARIO!" they all said.

"It's Gia's birthday? Oh no, I couldn't stop thinking about my birthday, and I forgot that hers is today! I didn't even buy a present," Mario said.

"But Mario, you spent the whole day with her. Gia's birthday is special because she got to spend time with her cousin," Nana said. "We are all so excited to celebrate both of your birthdays today."

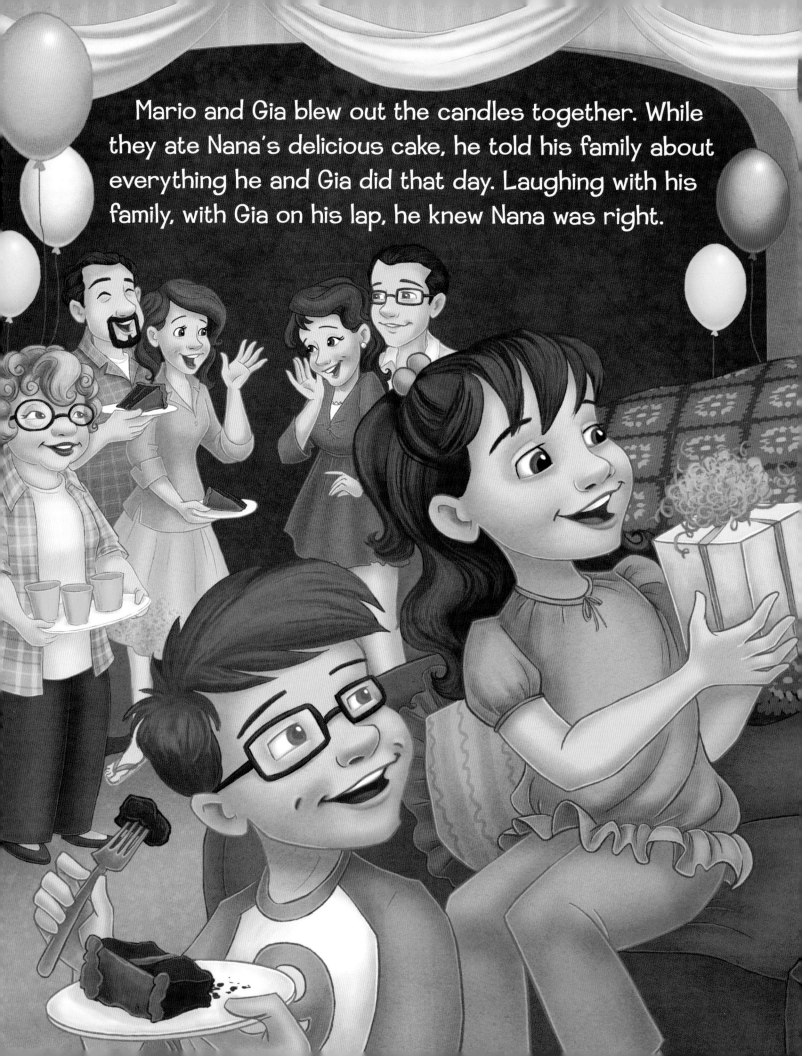

Mario and Gia blew out the candles together. While they ate Nana's delicious cake, he told his family about everything he and Gia did that day. Laughing with his family, with Gia on his lap, he knew Nana was right.

Family is the best gift of all.